Flap your wings
and you can fly,
higher and higher,
up, up in the sky.

# Hop, hop, hop!

Now swim along
and
stretch
up
your
neck.

Say
"Hello darling."

Then swoop like a starling.

Swoop
up

and
down,

Swoop round and round.

Scratch the ground with your feet.

Catch a fly with your beak.

Stand
very
tall
on
just
one
leg.

Say
"Cluck cluck!"
and lay an egg.

Catch
a
wriggly
Snake

and
stretch
out
your
wings.

Open your beak and

sing!

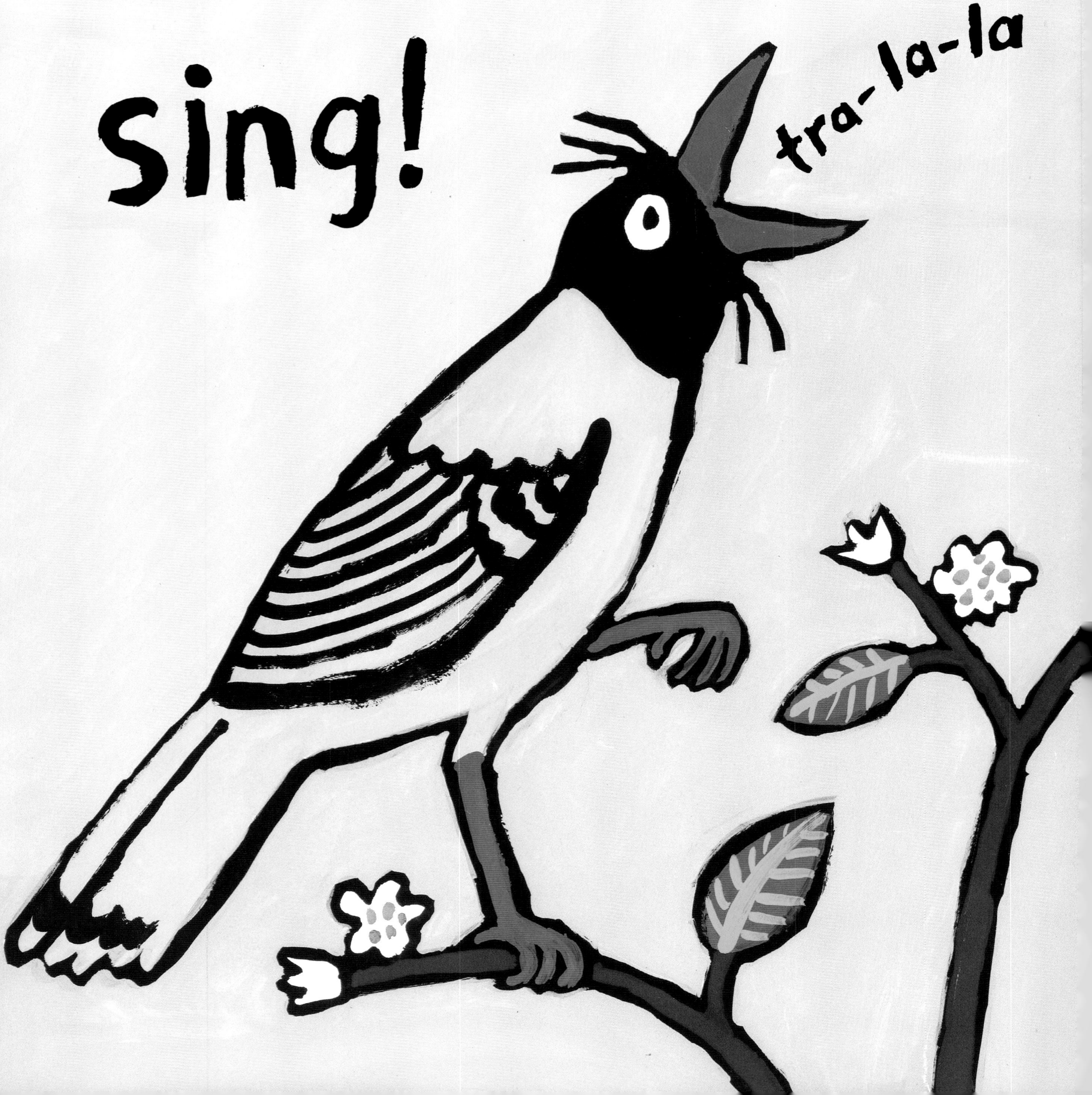

Waddle like a penguin in the snow.

Show off your tail

and
wiggle
your
bum.

Now sit in your
nest
and cuddle with
mum.

What a busy bird
you've been.
The funniest one
I've ever seen!

You began the day
Cock-a-doodle-doo!
Now say goodnight...